JANE YOLEN

How Do Dinosaurs Eat Their Food?

Illustrated by

MARK TEAGUE

How does a dinosaur
eat all his food?

Does he burp,

does he belch,

or make noises

quite rude?

Does he pick at his cereal,

throw down

his cup,

hoping to make someone else pick it up?

Does he fuss, does he fidget,
or squirm in his chair?

Does he flip his spaghetti

high into the air?

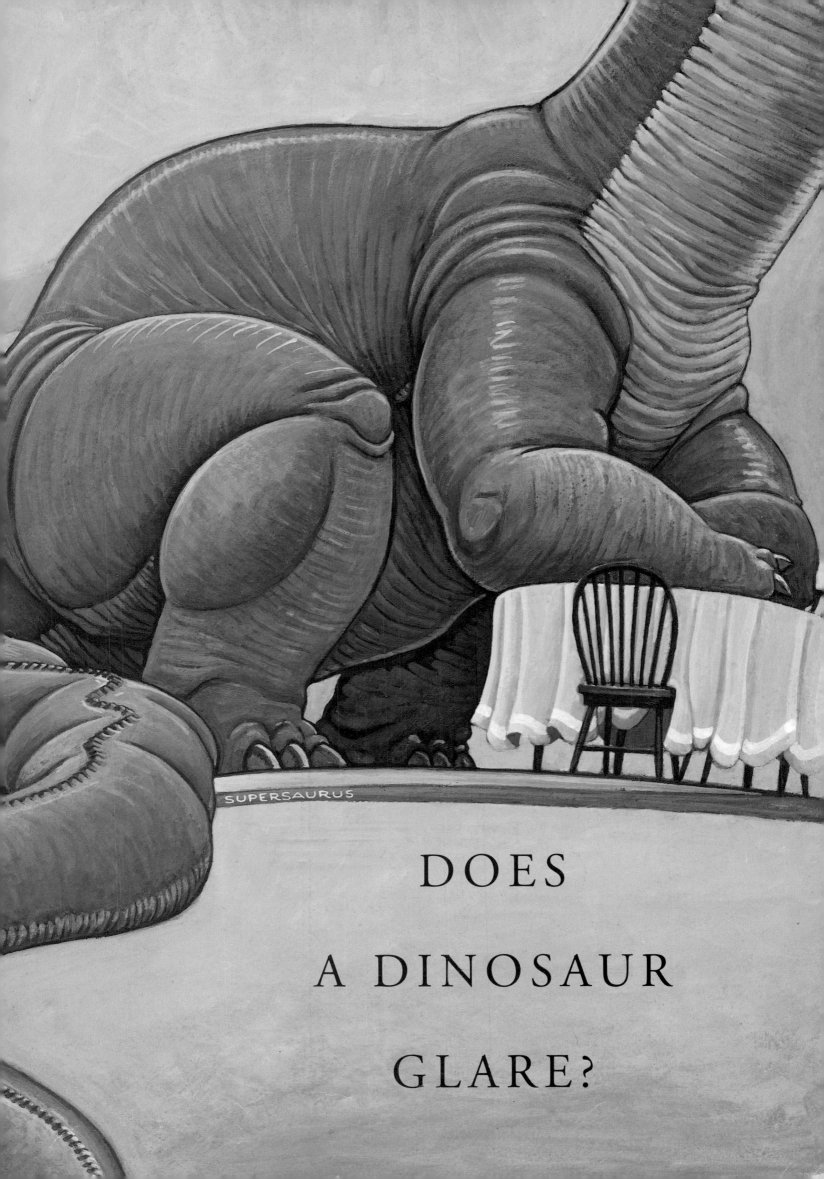

DOES

A DINOSAUR

GLARE?

How does a dinosaur
eat all his food?
Does he spit
out his broccoli
partially chewed?

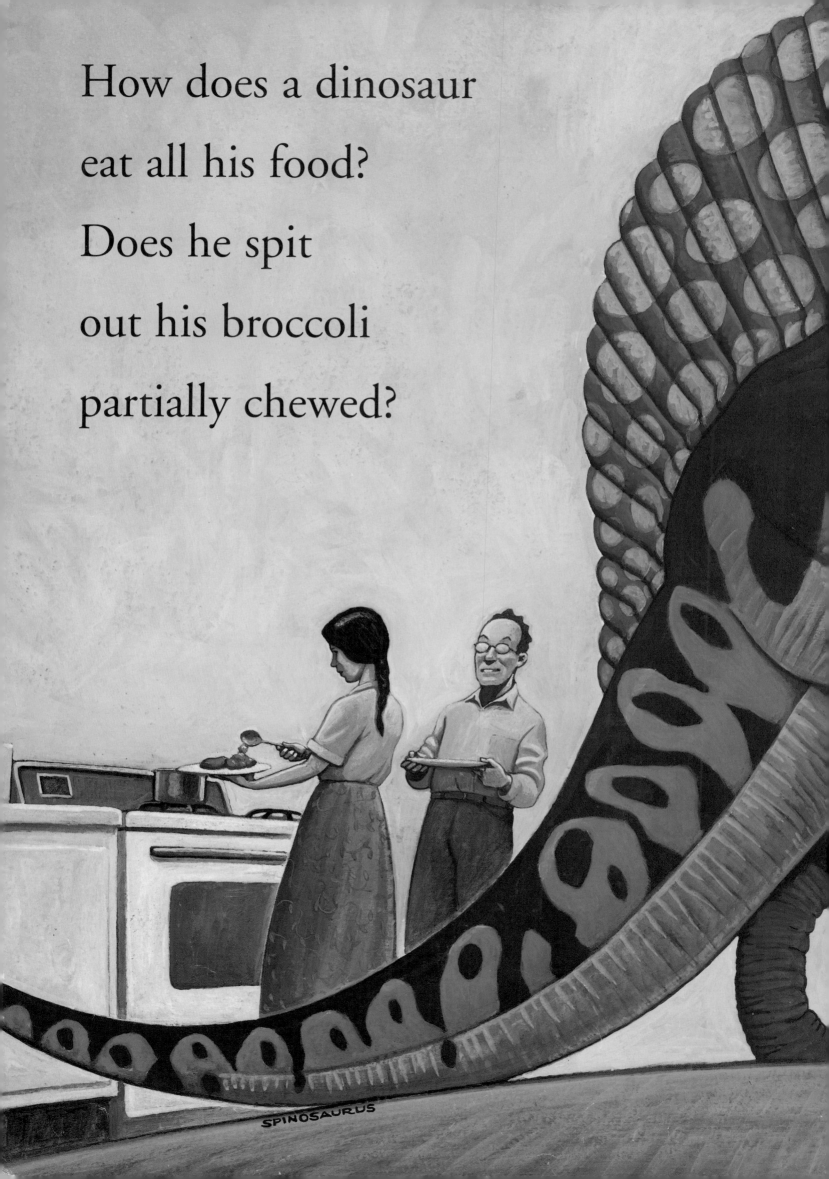

Does he bubble

his milk?

Stick beans

up his nose?

Does he squeeze juicy oranges

with his big toes?

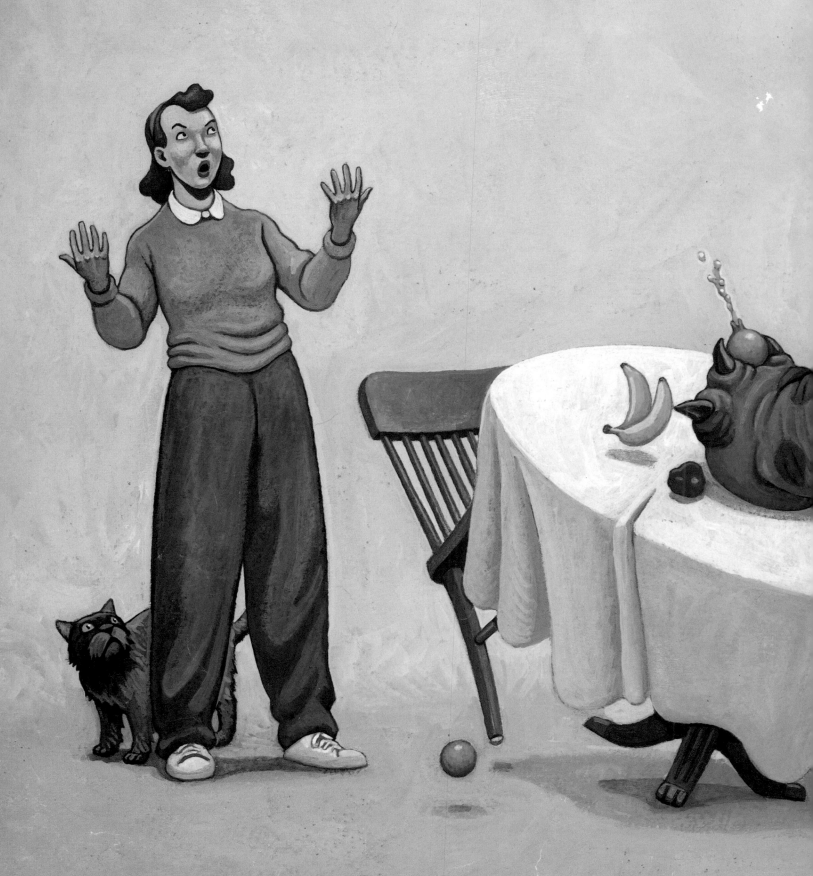

POLACANTHUS

No . . .

He says, "Please"

and "Thank you."
He sits very still.

He eats all before him
with smiles and goodwill.

He tries
every new thing,
at least one
small bite.

He makes
no loud noises –
that isn't polite.

He never
drops anything
on to the floor.
And after
he's finished,
he asks for
some more.

Eat up.

Eat up, little dinosaur.